Alma
and the
Magic Yo-Yo

This edition first published in Great Britain 1999 by Mammoth
First published in Great Britain 1996 by Heinemann Young Books
imprints of Egmont Children's Books Limited
239 Kensington High Street, London W8 6SA.
Published in hardback by Heinemann Library,
a division of Reed Educational and Professional Publishing Limited
by arrangement with Egmont Children's Books Limited.
Text copyright © David Sutherland 1996
Illustrations copyright © Philip Hopman 1996
Additional illustrations copyright © Philip Hopman 1999
The Author and Illustrator have asserted their moral rights.
Paperback ISBN 0 7497 3780 8
Hardback ISBN 0 431 06197 1
10 9 8 7 6 5 4 3 2 1
A CIP catalogue record for this title
is available from the British Library.
Printed at Oriental Press Limited, Dubai.

Alma and the Magic Yo-Yo

David Sutherland

Illustrated by Philip Hopman

 **YELLOW BANANAS**

For Camilla and Jasper

D.S.

To Maggie

P.H.

Chapter One

HAVE YOU EVER played with a yo-yo? A normal yo-yo that goes down when you throw it down, then comes spinning back up into your hand all by itself?

Clever, isn't it, the way a yo-yo does that?

You can throw it out in front of you and it will come straight back. You can throw it behind you. After a little practice, you can fling it up into the air and it will come spinning back down to you with the string all wound up nicely.

Amazing!

You can get whistling yo-yos, green hairy yo-yos, see-through yo-yos with electric lights inside, striped and spotted yo-yos, even fluorescent glow-in-the-dark yo-yos.

If you are interested in yo-yos (and I can see at once that you are!) I expect you will be especially interested in meeting my very good friend, Alma Rosetree.

Alma was the star pupil at the Yo-yo Academy, that world-famous college for the training of professional yo-yoists.

One day she was sitting in the courtyard, studying, when along came two girls from her class, Amy and Arabella.

'What a fab dress you're wearing, Alma! Is it new?' asked Amy.

Poor Alma blushed and looked down at her old rosy lacy frock. It was the only dress she owned and she had to wear it every day. Amy knew this very well and smiled cruelly to Arabella.

'I say, Alma, have you seen my new computer-designed, laser-guided, twin-turbo-powered yo-yo?' Arabella asked.

She took a walnut box, lined with red velvet, from her school bag. Inside was the finest yo-yo Alma had ever seen.

'Gosh!' she said. 'It's beautiful!'

'It was also extremely expensive,' Arabella confirmed, snatching it away before Alma could even touch it. 'Daddy bought it in America. There are only five like it in the world.'

Alma sighed. She knew she could never afford such a wonderful yo-yo. Her father had died when she was a baby and her mother had sold their little house in order to pay for her to go to the Yo-yo Academy.

'It must be wonderful to throw a yo-yo like that,' said Alma modestly.

'Oh, it's a dream! You might have done rather better at the French Open Championship if you'd had one of these instead of that clumsy old thing you've been using!'

Alma felt like crying. She shifted nervously on

the bench staring down at her shoes.

'Just watch this!' Arabella continued proudly. She slipped her finger into the loop and flicked a switch on the side of the yo-yo. It made a low purring sound and two green lights came on. Casually, she tossed it out in front of her in a throw called Walking the Dog.

The yo-yo made a high-pitched squeal as the first turbo fired. Then the second turbo went into overdrive, with the sound of a jet plane taking off! Arabella was jerked off her feet. She went flying across the courtyard on the end of her yo-yo string! CRASH! She landed in a hedge with her legs in the air. Poor Arabella.

Chapter Two

AS ALMA WALKED home that day, she thought hard about the future. Her father had been a champion yo-yoist. Her grandmother and her Great Uncle Horatio had been champion yo-yoists. (Here, in fact, is a picture of Alma's Great Uncle Horatio receiving the European Palme d'Or from the King of Antwerp in 1882.)

But, for Alma, now almost eight years old, success had always seemed so near, and yet so far. At the age of five she had narrowly missed winning the Prix de Rome. The next year she was tipped for an Olympic Gold Medal, but tragically sprained her wrist during the final heat. Earlier this year she was beaten into second place at the French Open. It was heartbreaking.

And now, in just a few days' time, she would face the greatest test of all: the once-in-a-lifetime chance to compete at the SUPER-MEGA YO-YO UNIVERSATHON in Hollywood, California. The winner would become Supreme Yo-yoist of the Universe!

All the top competitors would have their eyes on the glittering prize money. But Alma knew she had only one serious rival: the highly talented Pink Eddie Jinks.

Pink Eddie Jinks – several years her senior, elegant but cunning . . . throwing in the peculiar African Style – had always managed to beat Alma.

It was he who had won the Prix de Rome! It was he who had taken the Olympic Gold Medal! And now all of Paris was raving about Pink Eddie Jinks.

Alma remembered it all as if it were yesterday, as she practised her best and favourite throws outside the battered caravan where she lived with her mother.

If only she could win in Hollywood then she could afford to buy her mum a new house! There was nothing in the world she wanted more!

Chapter Three

IT WAS NOVEMBER and Alma Rosetree
shivered in her old rosy lacy frock, as she
changed the string on her best and favourite
yo-yo (the one she had come so close to
winning with in Paris).

Her mother called to her, 'Alma, love, leave
your yo-yo for five minutes and come and have
some tea!'

Alma joined her mother in the caravan. They
stirred their tea in silence. The next day they
would fly to California. Everything they had
lived for, planned for, dreamt of, depended
on Alma winning the Hollywood Yo-yo
Universathon. They had to be ready.

Alma's mother reached deep into the pocket
of her old pleated skirt, and took out a shabby,
but highly unusual, yo-yo.

'I want you to take this, Alma, love,' she said.
'It belonged to your dear Great Uncle Horatio.
He made me promise never to let you throw it,
but just keep it in your pocket for good luck in
Hollywood.'

'Why can't I throw it? Why can't I play with it?'

Alma's mother shook her head solemnly. 'It's too unpredictable. You never know what might happen with a yo-yo like that!'

Alma took the yo-yo and studied it carefully. Here was a yo-yo of truly great character. The sides were perfectly formed and it had excellent weight and balance. Its string, though old, was spun from the finest Egyptian cotton. On each side were carved three strange symbols which might have been part of some ancient alphabet – something to do with wizardry or alchemy . . . something deeply mysterious and magical!

'Where did it come from?' Alma asked her mother. 'Where did he get it?'

'It was given to him by a wise old man in India. No one knows how old it is or who made it.'

This was clearly a yo-yo to be taken seriously. Alma put it in the pocket of her rosy lacy frock. In Hollywood she would need all the luck she could get!

Chapter Four

IN CALIFORNIA THE sun is always shining and everyone seems to be on holiday. Everybody smiles and says, 'Hi!' Californians are the happiest people in the world!

Alma Rosetree was happy too; happy but excited – and more than a little nervous.

She was sitting with her mother in her dressing room at the Hollywood Yo-yo Stadium. On the walls around her were photos of the world's greatest yo-yoists: Slim Tim Buck-Tooth, Fat Flora Underbed, Willie 'The Wink' Watson.

Perhaps, thought Alma, one day my photo will be up there as well!

Alma's mother finished brushing her daughter's hair and stood back to inspect the result. Alma looked radiant! Her eyes shone with excitement and even her old rosy lacy frock somehow looked new.

There was still half an hour before the first contestants were due on stage. Alma carefully put her best and favourite competition yo-yo in the drawer of her dressing table and left the room with her mother to get some tea.

But in the hall, on their way to the cafeteria, who should they meet but Pink Eddie Jinks!

Alma's heart froze. She never expected to meet her great rival face to face!

Pink Eddie Jinks smiled his aristocratic but devious smile. Then he straightened the cuffs

of his famous pink shirt and made a low bow.
'Miss Rosetree, what a great pleasure,' he said.

Alma nodded her head in return and
squeezed past him in the narrow corridor.

Pink Eddie Jinks continued on his way. He
paused just outside Alma's dressing room,
watching carefully until Alma and her mother
had disappeared round the corner . . .

Chapter Five

'THERE'S SOMETHING I don't like about that Pink Eddie Jinks,' Alma's mother said as they sipped their tea.

'Oh, Mum, don't say that!' protested Alma. 'He's such a fine yo-yoist!'

Suddenly a great cheer rose up from the stadium. The contest was about to begin! Alma and her mother made their way to the edge of the stage to watch the first act.

The yo-yoist made some brave and delicate throws, but fumbled badly while attempting a Double-Twisting, Double-Back, Round-the-World and Through-the-Legs throw. His yo-yo clattered awkwardly to the floor.

The three very serious judges muttered and nodded and scratched their noses thoughtfully. They held up their score-cards: six out of ten; five out of ten; four out of ten. A total of fifteen out of a possible thirty. (Of course no one expects to score a perfect thirty; a perfect ten, ten, ten.)

One after another, the contestants tried their best to please the crowd and to impress the judges. But it was only when the great champion, Pink Eddie Jinks, took the stage that the audience really went wild.

And what a performance! Eddie Jinks (with his famous pink yo-yos) pulled out all the stops. Throwing in the African Style, he made one perfect yo-yo throw after another!

He threw two yo-yos at once – one in each hand! He threw *three* yo-yos at once – holding the string of the third between his teeth. He did three simultaneous Double-Twisting, Double-Back, Round-the-World and Through-the-Legs throws at once!

It was incredible.

The crowd were ecstatic. They'd never seen anything like it before!

'Oh Eddie,' sighed a young girl standing next to Alma. 'You're the best!'

A hush fell over the vast Yo-yo Stadium as

Pink Eddie Jinks smoothed back his shiny hair and straightened the cuffs of his famous pink shirt in preparation for his final throw: a fabulously difficult Double String Flip.

In this throw, you must flip the yo-yo into the air, letting go of the loop at the end of the string. Then, after it turns three circles in mid-air, you must catch the loop again on the tip of your finger. Pink Eddie Jinks was about to attempt this with two yo-yos at once!

The crowd held their breath. There was a roll of drums . . .

'He'll never do it!' someone muttered. 'It's impossible!'

He made the throw . . . He let go of the strings . . . the yo-yos made one, two, three circles and –

YES! He did it! He caught both the loops – a feat never before seen in all the glorious history of yo-yo competition!

The crowd went wild! They were out of control! They couldn't wait to see the judges' score cards! And there they were: ten out of ten; ten out of ten; nine out of ten!

Pink Eddie Jinks had just scored an unbelievable twenty-nine points out of thirty! How could Alma possibly hope to beat that?

She would now have to produce a perfect thirty
– a perfect ten, ten, ten, in order to win.

And no one – but *no one* – had ever done
that before.

Chapter Six

WITH A SINKING heart, Alma returned to her dressing room to collect her best and favourite yo-yo. 'That's it. I've lost,' she sighed. 'I can't possibly win. How can I? How can I beat Pink Eddie Jinks' twenty-nine?'

She thought of all the work she had put in over the last year, preparing for just this moment. She thought of the great sacrifices her dear mother had made.

She thought of their dream of buying a little house, if only she could win . . . she thought of returning to live in the leaky caravan if she lost . . .

All these thoughts went through Alma's mind as she opened the door to her dressing room.

She crossed the room to the drawer where she had left her yo-yo.

She opened the drawer. She looked in the drawer and her face turned a ghostly white. Her knees went weak. Her heart missed a beat.

Alma looked and looked again, but the drawer was quite empty.

Alma Rosetree was due on stage at the SUPER-MEGA YO-YO UNIVERSATHON in just three minutes and her best and favourite competition yo-yo was missing!

'But how could this happen?' she asked herself. 'How could this possibly happen?'

Alma sat down in the only chair and buried her face in her hands. Salty tears ran through her fingers and fell in dark wet circles on her rosy lacy frock. Her greatest dream was utterly shattered.

Suddenly a blast of cold air flooded the dressing room.

Alma looked up and gasped.

There, in the mirror, staring out at her, all pale and ghostly, was the face of her Great Uncle Horatio. His lips began to move. He was speaking to her.

'Take my yo-yo and have faith, Alma Rosetree. You are destined to do great things on the awesome and glittering stage of yo-yo history! Have faith, Alma Rosetree!'

Her Great Uncle's voice echoed eerily in the icy room but by the time she had dried her eyes, the face had vanished.

Alma looked all around. She was quite alone. She reached into the pocket of her rosy lacy frock and took out her Great Uncle's ancient yo-yo. Thoughtfully she passed her finger over the mysterious, carved symbols.

Just then the door to her room burst open and her mother shouted, 'Alma, love, don't dawdle, dear. It's your turn. You're on. Hurry up!'

Alma stood, shakily, then made her way towards the stage.

The crowd were clapping and shouting and the roar was deafening. The footlights were dazzling as Alma took the stage. In her hand was an untested and unpredictable yo-yo, a strange and ancient yo-yo which she had never thrown before.

She stood in the spotlight. It was so quiet Alma could hear her own heart-beat. All eyes were upon her. In the wings, Pink Eddie Jinks smiled his aristocratic but devious smile.

Alma decided to begin with a few ordinary straight down and up throws, just to get warmed up.

She hooked her finger in the loop . . . She flicked her wrist. She threw the yo-yo . . .

Suddenly all 93,000 people in the stadium gasped! All together they jumped to their feet for a better view, for what they were seeing was too amazing to be believed!

Instead of Alma Rosetree staying in one place and the yo-yo going down and up, the yo-yo stayed still in mid-air.

Alma Rosetree was going up and down and round and round on the end of the string!

The crowd roared their approval! They went berserk! They chanted and stamped their feet and threw their programmes in the air!

'That's my daughter! That's my Alma!' shouted Alma's mother.

The judges mumbled to each other and consulted the Official Yo-yo Rule Book. Never before had they had to rule on such a strange performance. Alma's heart was beating like a drum as she waited for their decision.

Finally the first judge stood and held up her score-card. *It was a ten.*

The second judge stood. Ten again!

The third judge shook his head. He scowled and muttered and combed his fingers through his grey hair. No one had ever been awarded a triple ten before.

Slowly he rose . . . He held up his card. It was a *nine and a half!*

She'd done it. *She'd won!* Alma Rosetree had just become the *Supreme Yo-yoist of the Universe!*

Chapter Seven

THE NEXT DAY, Alma and her mother flew
back to England with their prize money. They
bought a sweet little house and painted it inside
and out. They put yo-yo-patterned wallpaper in
Alma's room. They planted tulips and forget-
me-nots in the garden and put a little white
fence around it. Alma had never been happier
in her life.

Outside the house a great crowd of reporters

gathered, all eager for an interview with the new champion.

'Miss Rosetree, have you considered entering politics?' asked one, as she appeared on the doorstep.

'What about the offer of hosting a new television chat show?'

'Any truth in the rumour of a romance between you and Pink Eddie Jinks?'

Alma answered 'No' firmly to all these questions and told the journalists that she simply planned to go back to school and catch up on all the things she'd missed.

And so, on the first day of the school term (in a brand new rosy lacy frock), Alma skipped happily down the stairs for breakfast. As she reached the hall, a small packet clunked noisily through the letterbox. What could it be? Who was it from? Alma went to look.

It was addressed to her. Quickly she opened it and – there inside – was her own best and favourite competition yo-yo, the very one that had gone missing in Hollywood! But no letter. Not a word of explanation.

Alma sat thoughtfully through breakfast, wondering, *Where on earth could this have come from?*

But then she put it to one side and went back to her cornflakes. After all, there is more to life than yo-yos and Alma Rosetree felt she had already experienced more than her share of ups and downs.

The End

Yellow Bananas are bright, funny, brilliantly imaginative stories written by some of today's top writers. All the books are beautifully illustrated in full colour.

So if you've enjoyed this story, why not pick another from the bunch?

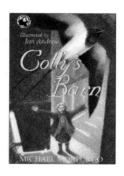